MISS OPAL MAKES A MATCH

A Miss Opal Story

Book 1

AMY K. ROGNLIE

Miss Opal Makes a Match
© 2016 by Amy K. Rognlie
All rights reserved.

This story is set in Bell County, Texas. Located in south Central Texas, Bell County was founded in 1850 and is rich in historical significance. Though this book is a work of fiction, the location and places mentioned are real and are described, to the best of my knowledge, with historically accurate details. Names, characters, events, and incidents are the product of the author's imagination or are used fictitiously. Any resemblance to actual events or persons, living or dead, is coincidental.

ISBN: 978-1-53999-794-8

Chapter One

1907, Belton, Texas

As close as she could reckon, Opal Wilson had been talking to the Lord pretty near every day of her eighty-one years. And when He spoke, she listened.

Though the sun had just barely grazed the horizon, Opal found her sister in the kitchen already, whipping up a batch of fluffy biscuits. Armilda wasn't much for shirking, as their Papa always said.

Opal watched her sister from the doorway. Armilda's hair, unlike her own, still had streaks of rich black threaded here and there through the silver, and its soft waves fit its owner's personality. Really, neither of them were getting any younger, but until God saw fit to call them home to heaven, there was work to be done here in their own little corner of Texas.

Opal thumped the water bucket down onto the chair. "We've got to do something about the preacher, Armilda."

Her sister nodded. "And fast. Do you have any ideas?"

"Yes, ma'am! I've been praying on it a good while. See this newspaper right here?"

****

1907, near Marble Falls, Texas

Lyna Marshall yanked her valise off of the bed and took one last glance around her room. Though small, she would miss it. She still couldn't believe she had agreed to this. Leave her ranch and her family for three whole months? To care for a couple of elderly women whom she didn't know? She'd never been away from home before.

When she had first seen the advertisement in the *Austin Statesman and Tribune*, she had thought it was too good to be true.

Wanted: Single woman to care for elderly sisters in their home. Three months. Must be Christian, age 18-24, able to play the piano. Bonus for good singing voice. Room and board plus $250 per month. Please respond to Miss Opal Wilson, Belton, Texas.

She fit all of the criteria...but still. What if the sisters were too ill for her to care for them? She was used to hard work, but she didn't know much about tending to the sick. And what if they wanted her to cook? Pa and Jacob had gotten used to her limited skills, but cooking for others would be different. She grimaced.

But she couldn't pass up the money. Two hundred and fifty dollars a month! Pa and Jacob could get along without her for three months for that kind of money. She would be able to pay off the last of the debt on the ranch, and then Pa wouldn't have to work so hard—and maybe she would be free to see what God had planned for her life.

She knew He had a plan. She had sensed it even as a small child while saying her prayers at night or listening to Pa's deep voice reading from the family Bible. And as she grew older, she heard His voice calling to her during those long, quiet hours riding the range with Jacob—perceived His creativity in the grandeur of the rolling prairie and the never-fading verdant green of the live oak trees. Often, she rode by herself to the ridge that overlooked their neighbor's land. From her vantage point, the never-ending fields of cotton were like a blanket of snow in summer. White unto harvest.

So maybe she would become a missionary to deepest, darkest Africa, like…like David Livingstone, the brave Scottish doctor.

She would travel for miles and miles across barren prairielands and treacherous mountains, braving dust storms and tornados and bandits until she reached California. Then she would board a rickety old ship and set sail for Africa, with only her Bible and one small trunk, full of all of her worldly possessions. Of course, she would probably be shipwrecked on the way because that always happened to the poor missionaries whom she had read about. But a dashing, dark-haired sailor would rush to her rescue and then—

"Lyna!" her brother hollered from downstairs.

"I'm coming!" Ready or not, her adventure had begun. "Be thou my vision," she murmured.

****

Rev. Andrew Marek drummed his fingers on the wagon seat. He had never thought of himself as an impatient person, but he only had so many hours in a day. And waiting here outside the Wilson's house in the heat for an hour was not helping. Miss Opal was probably wondering why he had not come inside to wait, but truth be told, he didn't want to be around Margaret any more than he had to at this point.

He hated feeling this way, but he was in over his head. That's just all there was to it. Pastoring a circuit of four small churches was difficult to begin with, but now he had Margaret to deal with. At least she was leaving today and wouldn't return to Texas until almost time for their wedding—three months from now. He gulped. He was getting married to Margaret. In three months.

He pictured her large, doe-like eyes, her trim figure, and her golden-blonde hair. Any man with eyes in his head would take a second look at his fiancée. But—

She poked her head out the front door. "I'm almost ready, Andrew dear."

He fidgeted on the wagon seat as she disappeared back into the house. It was already 1:45. What could be taking so long, for crying out loud?

Patience. He was always preaching to others about having patience. He blew out a breath. Clearly, he wasn't following his own advice today. But he'd already hefted three large trunks and two bags into the wagon, not to mention the dratted bassoon in its enormous case. She was leaving on the 3:05 train, and it was at least an hour drive into Temple.

And he was supposed to be picking up some relative of the Wilson sisters while he was at the train station. A niece, maybe? He couldn't remember what Miss Opal had said, but he fervently hoped that she was a quiet woman. He couldn't take much more chatter.

Twenty minutes later, Margaret finally emerged in a fancy purple gown, dressed as if she were headed to a personal audience with President Roosevelt instead of a dusty five-day train journey across the country. In August.

"I can't believe I'm heading back to Boston just in time for the debutante balls." She clutched his sleeve. "I wish you were going with me, Andrew."

Not on your life, darlin'.

He nodded to Miss Opal and Miss Armilda, who were standing on the porch, waving off their guest.

"Three months will go by quickly, no doubt," he said, not looking at her. He clucked to the horses, and they were on their way. Finally.

What was wrong with him? He would soon be married to a beautiful woman from one of Boston's leading families, and yet he felt as though he were willingly walking to the gallows. Did all men feel this way before their weddings?

She raised her finely-tweezed eyebrows. "You don't sound very happy about it."

That was astute. And the first time she had noticed his feelings for the whole three weeks she had been here.

"Just a lot on my mind, Margaret." He patted her gloved hand. "I'm sure you'll be busy with preparations and the time will fly by. You'll be back before you know it."

She cocked her head to the side like his dog did when he was trying to understand the human words. "In three months," she repeated.

He nodded wearily. Hadn't they already established that about ten times? He wished he could drum up some of the feelings he'd had for her a year or two ago. But something had changed. The feelings had faded away. He could see that now.

Margaret sighed and pulled her hand away to straighten her hat.

Andrew glanced at it out of the corner of his eye. A ridiculous thing, covered in flowers and … fake birds. Why would a woman wear something like that?

She scooted closer to him. "Andrew, dear—"

The whiny tone in her voice made him grit his teeth. He knew what was coming next.

"I know we've discussed this before, darling, but why can't you move back to Boston? You could be a pastor of a large church there, and wouldn't have to work yourself into exhaustion like you are now, in this dusty, God-forsaken—" She apparently had a rare flash of good sense and stopped midsentence, only to forge ahead again. "We could have a lovely home near the waterfront, and my father—"

"I'm not going back to Boston, Margaret."

If she thought he was going to subject himself to her father again, she was wrong. And besides, Texas was home now.

She stuck her rouged lip out. "Well. Maybe you'll change your mind while I'm gone. If you loved me, you'd move back to Boston."

The whiny voice again.

Resisting the urge to tell her that if *she* loved *him,* she wouldn't ask him to, he shrugged. He would not feel guilty. God had called him to this place and these people, and her pouting wasn't going to change that. Nothing he said made her understand.

"We're almost to the train station, Margaret. Let's not argue anymore." He turned the horses from the lane to the main road. "Please send me a telegram when you arrive home, so I know you're there safely."

Chapter Two

Margaret's leaving left a blessed silence in its wake.

"Good heavens," Opal said, dropping into her rocking chair.

There seemed to be nothing more that could be said at that moment.

The sisters rocked in unison for long minutes, their ladder-back rockers squeaking amiably on the white-washed boards of the front porch. The whir of the cicadas blared and ebbed, blared and ebbed again in the close heat of the August afternoon.

Opal pressed her icy glass of mint tea against her cheek.

A slight breeze set the hanging ferns swaying, and sparrows flitted in and out of the largest one, fashioning their newest nest. The sweet smell of the Confederate jasmine wafted through the air.

Armilda's sigh broke the silence. "The bassoon-playing was the worst."

Opal nodded, her eyes closed. "I could have borne the bassoon practice. But she prattled on and on like that ridiculous parrot at the mercantile. Why, Mother would have been mortified if either of us had carried on like that."

"And not a lick of sense in the girl's head." Armilda sniffed.

They continued rocking.

"Good thing we have a plan." Opal opened one eye to look at her sister.

The sisters grinned at each other.

"We have two hours before Andrew returns with Miss Marshall." Opal rose and set her tea glass down. She bent to do a few energetic toe-touches, then reached for the cane she had purchased the day before. "Shall we commence?"

****

Lyna pinched the bridge of her nose. The novelty of the train ride had worn off an hour ago, and the middle-aged woman in the seat next to her had been chattering since Austin, where they had both boarded the northbound train to Temple on the "The Katy"— the Missouri, Kansas and Texas Railroad line.

Poor woman must not have anyone to talk to. But she was a fount of information about Belton, where Lyna would be living for the next three months.

"I'm staying with the Wilson sisters," Lyna inserted when the woman stopped for a breath. "Do you know them?"

"Oh, my, yes. Everyone knows Miss Opal and Miss Armilda. Are they fetching ya from the train station? Or are ya takin' the trolley out to Belton?"

"I didn't know there was a trolley. Miss Opal said she'd send—"

"Yes, ma'am! Only one a' three trolleys in the whole wide state of Texas. Called the Temple-Belton Interurban Trolley." The woman pronounced the name carefully, like a small child trying out a new word. "Finished it a year or two ago. Even built a big ol' bridge so's it could go right over the Leon River. Never seen anything like it. Ya shoulda seen the big to-do on the first day!"

"I can imagine," Lyna murmured.

But no imagination was necessary, it turned out. Mrs. Chatter Box filled her in on every last detail. By the time Lyna's train pulled into the Katy Depot in Temple, her head was throbbing. She hadn't realized how much she enjoyed the quiet solitude of her life on the ranch.

"Maybe I'll meet up with ya in Belton one day," her new friend said over her shoulder as they struggled down the narrow aisle with their luggage.

Lyna grimaced. Or maybe not. She followed the woman through the train door, then paused to survey the scene. The flat strip of hard-packed dirt that served as both the boarding and departure area was full of folks chatting, laughing, hugging. Surprised at the sudden sense of excitement coursing through her, Lyna stopped herself from bolting down the train steps. She must remember to act like a lady now, not a ranch hand. Her momentary homesickness had fled as soon as she exited the train. When had she ever been on an adventure by herself?

"All aboard for the 3:01 train, departing to Dallas!"

Amid the commotion, a young couple caught Lyna's attention. The man, tall and dark, towered over a blond woman who appeared to be headed to a very fancy event.

Lyna couldn't tear her gaze away from the woman's hat. A huge thing made from purple velvet and covered in flowers and...*birds*? *Was that the style nowadays*? Her own best Sunday straw hat and green gingham dress felt plain in comparison.

The man bent to peck the woman's cheek, and she flung her arms around his neck, clinging to him in the most romantic manner.

Lyna clasped her hands to her chest.

One day, someone would hold her in his arms like that. She would rapturously gaze into his dark mysterious eyes under heavenly-scented roses cascading down over an arbor that—

The man had disentangled himself and now stood facing the woman. He didn't seem very pleased. Why was he scowling at her?

And why was the young woman leaving her grumpy beau? Maybe she was traveling back east, to comfort her mother who lay dying of a terrible disease. No, no. She was too gussied up for that. So maybe she was heading to the coast ... maybe to

Galveston. Maybe she was a nurse, and she was going to help the—no, no. She secretly worked for the government, and she was on her way to carry some important papers across the country. The colossal hat would be the perfect place to conceal papers.

Lyna's train of thought screeched to a halt when tears rolled down the young woman's cheeks.

Definitely not a government agent. Probably dying mother.

Such a shame. Lyna turned away to give the woman privacy in her grief. She couldn't believe someone would carry on like that in public, but who was she to say? The poor woman must be overwrought.

Lyna glanced around for the person who was supposed to pick her up. What was the man's name again?

Marek. Opal had written that a Mr. Marek would meet her at the Temple depot and escort her to Belton. Dark hair. Blue wagon. Why hadn't Miss Opal given her more information? How was she to find a man with so little to go on?

At least fifteen wagons, several of them blue, were parked helter-skelter on both sides of the tracks. She switched her valise to her other hand and threaded her way through the crowd to the flickering shade of a young hackberry tree. She would just have to wait and let the man find her.

It was still dreadfully hot in Central Texas in August, but not as hot as last year. She pulled off her gloves and stowed them in her valise. She wasn't used to wearing them on the ranch and hoped it wasn't too much of a breach of etiquette to be bare-handed at the train station.

Her thoughts drifted toward home. Hopefully, they'd have a few good rains once September rolled around. By now, the tanks were nearly dry of the moisture that had fallen in the spring, and the cattle would have a rough go of it if it was an arid autumn. But—she didn't have to worry about that right now. Pa, Jacob, and the hands could take care of the ranch. They didn't need her.

She had her own job to do now. What would the two sisters be like? Miss Opal Wilson had sounded pleasant enough in her letter but had never said why the sisters needed Lyna's help. Were they both invalids? Or had they been ill recently and were just now recovering? Maybe they were just very old and frail and would need her to do everyday things like help them bathe and eat. Well, she would do whatever was required of her. And if she didn't know how to do it, she would learn. That's how Mama had raised her.

Andrew exhaled loudly as Margaret's train huffed out of the depot. These last three weeks had definitely not been what he had expected. Apparently, he and Margaret had grown further apart than he had thought since he had moved to Texas. He didn't remember her being so shallow … so self-centered.

She had long professed her love for him, even when as children their families lived next door to each other. He still had a vivid recollection of the time their families had vacationed together at the beach. He was fifteen, and Margaret was fourteen. Out on the boardwalk, surrounded by throngs of beachgoers, he managed to kiss her on the cheek without either of their fathers noticing.

But Margaret had changed and so had he. He rolled his head to stretch the kinks out of his neck. He felt stuck. Trapped.

But maybe it was just that she was not used to Texas yet. It was very different from Boston, that was for sure.

He glanced around, hoping he still had a moment to gather himself before he picked up Opal's guest. But she had likely disembarked earlier from the same northbound train that Margaret had just boarded and was no doubt already waiting for him. He half-wished he hadn't offered to help. He had just dealt with Margaret for almost a month, and a quiet wagon ride home—without a woman—would have been nice.

And the servant of the Lord must not strive; but be gentle unto all, apt to teach, patient…. The text of last week's sermon floated gently into his mind, like a dandelion seed on the wind. *Don't strive. Have patience. Rest in the Lord.* Sometimes a preacher needed his own sermon more than anyone else, that was for sure.

Andrew lifted his hat and wiped the sweat from his brow, as if to erase the bad humor that had gripped him lately. It wouldn't be fair to Opal's guest to be met by a crab bucket instead of his usual good-natured self.

He resettled his hat. Tomorrow would be back to normal, and he wouldn't have to deal with Margaret for three months. That alone was enough to make him smile.

He scanned the area for the woman Miss Opal had described. *Small, with reddish hair and a green dress. And a dimple.*

There. That must be her under the tree. Well, she was certainly small. He had been under the impression that he was meeting a young lady, not a child. He strode toward her.

"Miss Marshall?"

She tilted her head to look up at him from under the brim of her straw hat, and his throat constricted. Her wide, green gaze caught his and held for a long second. Definitely not a child.

"Mr. Marek?" She held out her hand.

He took it in his, and his skin tingled as her ungloved, work-roughened hand touched his. What was wrong with him? He had just sent off his fiancée, and here he was acting the fool over a woman he had just met.

What an idiot. He released her hand.

"Miss Opal…I mean, the Wilsons sent me to fetch you." As if she hadn't already figured that out.

She smiled. "Yes, she told me to watch for you. Is it far to where they live?"

He shook his head to clear it. "Only about an hour. Do you have a trunk?"

"Yes, just a small one." She gestured toward the depot. "Is it always this crowded here?"

"This is a quiet day. Wait until the cotton crop starts coming in this fall. Then you'll see crowded." He hoisted her trunk on his shoulder. "The farmers bring in bales and bales of the stuff for the Saturday cotton market."

"Our neighbors grow cotton." She trailed behind him as he strode toward the wagon.

He slowed his pace and grinned at her. "Pretty much everybody around here serves King Cotton. Unless they're railroad employees."

She accepted his help up into the wagon. "Papa tried farming cotton, but he likes running cattle instead."

They fell silent as they jounced over the dirt streets of Temple. It was always a rough ride through town, but he avoided the ruts the best he could. He glanced at Miss Marshall a couple of times, watching her face as she took in the sights. By now, Margaret would have talked enough to last him an entire day.

"Oh, it that a library?" She clasped her hands together. "It's so beautiful!"

He eyed the ornate building, with its elaborate rotunda and imposing columns.

"Yes, ma'am." He slowed the wagon as they drove past and assumed the droning voice of a tour guide. "The Carnegie Library, opened in 1904. The pride and joy of Tanglefoot, Texas—otherwise known as Temple."

"Tanglefoot?"

"That's what the locals call it. That or Mudtown."

She raised her eyebrows, as if she were trying to decide whether to take him seriously.

"Believe me, the names are quite appropriate," he said. "The streets are so bad after it rains that sometimes people abandon their wagons for a couple of days until the mud dries up." He slowed the horses to a walk as they neared the trolley tracks. "Have you never been to this area before, Miss Marshall?"

"No." She pushed stray wisps of hair from her forehead. "I live with my family on our ranch out near Marble Falls, and I've never ventured far. This was my first time to ride a train."

Family?

He glanced at her empty ring finger, then smiled at her enthusiasm. "A bit dusty though, aren't they? Train rides, I mean."

She shrugged. "No dustier than roundin' up the cattle. What's your occupation, Mr. Marek?"

"Well, today I'm a cab driver, I guess." His shoulders relaxed at the ease of conversation with this woman. "But usually I'm making the rounds between my churches. I'm a preacher."

She turned to stare at him. "You are?"

That was a different reaction. Usually, people would either squint and change the subject, or they would relate their entire life story. Not that he minded, of course. It came with the calling.

But he did wish she would stop gazing at him like…like he had done something amazing.

"I have four churches. The main one is in Belton, but I also travel to Flat, Little River, and Sparks."

Her eyes brightened. "My grandfather was a circuit preacher in New England. He died before I was born, but I've heard so many stories."

"I'd like to hear some of them sometime." He couldn't believe he had said that. He had just disentangled himself from Margaret—at least temporarily, and now he was encouraging this woman to tell him stories? "How long will you be visiting the Wilsons?"

"I'll be staying for three months. Unless they need me longer, I guess."

Need her?

"Tell me again how you are related to Miss Opal and Miss Armilda."

She gave him a blank look. "I'm not related to them. I've never met them before. I'm just coming to help take care of them."

What? She was coming to take care of *Opal* and *Armilda?* That would be the day. He pictured the two irrepressible old ladies. They could outwork him any day of the week.

He studied Miss Marshall from the corner of his eye. Surely she had misunderstood.

Or maybe *he* had misunderstood. As someone who dealt with people all of the time, he thought he was a pretty good judge of character, and this woman sitting next to him seemed genuine. Could she have ulterior motives for visiting the Wilsons?

When he had first arrived in Texas two years ago, they had opened their home to an idealistic but poor preacher, cheerfully treating him as if he were their long-lost relative. Even after he found his own place to stay, he continued to be a regular at the Wilson's dinner table. And he wasn't the only one. The sisters' generosity was well-known in the community, and he wouldn't want to see them taken advantage of—by anyone.

Well, he would find out soon enough. If Miss Marshall was going to be staying for several months, he would just have to keep an eye on her. Not that that would be much of a hardship.

He would not be distracted by a pair of remarkable green eyes, nor a set of adorable dimples.

He kept his eyes fixed between the horse's ears. And besides, he was practically married to Margaret. That thought stopped all others cold.

****

Lyna reined in her wayward emotions. Trouble. This preacher was going to be trouble. She had heard of love at first sight and had scoffed at the idea. But somehow, the minute those dark eyes had met hers, she was sunk. She had felt a—a connection like she had never felt with anyone else.

And he was a preacher. All of her life, she had heard the stories of how God had used her grandfather to reach people with the gospel as he galloped over miles and miles, crisscrossing New England many times in his zeal. Even as a child, she had longed to be part of that somehow and had secretly dreamed that maybe one day she would marry a man like her grandfather. It would be so exciting to ride horseback across the country. Meeting new people, learning new ideas, preaching the Good News to those in need—all with the man she loved. Whomever that might turn out to be.

She snuck another glance at Mr. Marek, surprised to find his gaze on her. She flushed and bent down to fiddle with her shoe lace.

Stop acting like child. Her first time off the ranch and she was fancying herself in love. And she wasn't even to Belton yet. Once she got there, she would have a job to do. She wouldn't have time to be mooning over a man.

And besides, hadn't she just seen him embracing another young lady on the train station platform? She was sure it had been him. She shrugged. She wasn't forward enough to ask, and it wasn't any of her business.

Chapter Three

Opal peered through the parlor window, then turned to call to her sister. "They ought to be here any time now, Armilda."

"I'm almost ready!" Armilda's voice sounded muffled, as if she were pulling her dress over her head.

Opal peeked out the window again. The parlor had always been the best place to wait for guests. Though not exactly cool, today the room felt slightly less hot than the kitchen, where the peach cobbler still bubbled in the oven. More importantly, one could see all the way up and down Main Street from this window. One must stay informed about the comings and goings of one's own town, after all.

They'd be here any moment, and it wouldn't do to be seen in her apron. Opal felt for her apron strings. Was it her imagination, or was she reaching further around her waist than usual to reach them? She hadn't done her daily constitutional exercises lately, what with all of the excitement going on around here, not to mention the bassoon-playing. She sighed. She was certainly paying now for her lack of self-discipline.

She stepped away from the window, still fishing for the apron ties. She should have never eaten those

Scottish Fancies at the Wednesday Women's Club meeting the other day, even if they were Evelyn Morrison's great-great-grandmother's most prized cookie recipe. The good Lord said that a person given to gluttony should be ashamed of herself.

Well, she'd just make sure not to eat any cobbler tonight. She sucked in her stomach and worked the whole apron around her waist until she could untie the stubborn knot from the front, then froze when she heard the rattle of a wagon. After all of this planning, she couldn't be caught still wearing her apron. She whooshed out her breath when she recognized the rattle as Mr. Jenkins' old cart. He always arrived home from working in the cotton mill about this time. And besides, the preacher's wagon had a more clattery-jingly sound to it than Horace Jenkins'.

Opal had finally freed herself from the apron when Armilda clumped through the door in her most unbecoming dress, the awful maroon satin she usually wore to funerals. She settled herself in her new chair and arranged her skirts.

"How do I look?"

Opal swept her up and down with a critical gaze. "Most untidy, Sister," she said cheerfully.

Armilda cocked an eyebrow.

"Disheveled, even," Opal said, grinning.

"Perfect." Armilda gave a satisfied nod.

****

Belton must be a wonderful place to live, Lyna decided as Mr. Marek guided the horses into the small town.

"How many people live here?" she asked.

"Oh, about four thousand, I'd guess."

Four thousand people. That was bigger than anywhere she'd ever been, except for the few times she had gone to Austin, and now Temple, of course. She spotted several churches, a dry goods store, and—

"And there's a library, here, too, though not quite as grand as the one in Temple." Mr. Marek pointed across the street.

The tan-colored brick building was graced with a band of fancy, diamond-pattern brown brick above the sign that said "Carnegie Library." Six large windows on each side of the double doors invited her to stop and peek inside. She could picture herself climbing up the stone steps, pulling open the intricately-carved door and basking in the glorious thought of all of those books that were just waiting to be read. Shelves and shelves of them.

"I didn't know there would be a library right here in town." She gripped the wagon seat and craned her neck around for a better view of the columned building as they left it behind. "I've never actually been inside of one before."

Mr. Marek raised his eyebrows. "You really haven't been off your ranch in a while, have you?"

She shook her head, wordless. *A library.* Right in the same town where she would be living for the next three months. What other wonderful surprises would this day hold?

A few blocks past the library, Mr. Marek pulled the horses to a stop in front of a large, white Victorian-style house on Main Street. An ancient live oak cast shadows over the spacious front yard, and purple heart vines spilled out of a bed by the limestone walkway. Beautiful sunburst designs graced the gables, and fancy fish-tail shingles crowned the well-kept home, while a tidy barn peeked out from behind the house. Best of all was an enormous bed of yellow daisies that flowed along the entire span of the white picket fence and separated the property from their neighbors'.

"Welcome to the Daisy Patch Inn." Mr. Marek gestured grandly toward the house. "What do you think?"

Inn? Lyna had envisioned something … smaller. More rundown. But this—this was so elegant. She could already picture herself ensconced in one of those white rockers on the wraparound porch, working her way through an entire pile of novels she had borrowed from the library.

"Is it truly an inn? It's much more grand than I'd imagined." Her fingers itched to pick some of those daisies. A huge bouquet of them would look grand on that little table on the front porch.

He chuckled. "No, not really. But I started calling it that when I used to live here, and I guess the name stuck."

She liked the sound of his laugh. "I'm anxious to meet the Wilsons."

"I'm sure they're eager to meet you as well. In fact, I'm surprised they weren't outside waiting for us."

"I think it's a little too warm out for that." She imagined two stoop-shouldered women, languishing in the humid heat as they waited for their new house help to arrive.

She gripped the handle of her valise and sat staring at the Wilson's house as Mr. Marek tied the horses. Was this all a dream? A handsome man, who just happened to be a preacher, had swooped her up and carried her away to a lovely little town, full of flowers and books and beauty. She sighed as she spotted a blue jay hopping along a branch of the Wilson's oak tree, his cerulean feathers brilliant against the dark green foliage. His sudden loud call intruded upon Lyna's consciousness, and she held her breath, sensing an undercurrent of...something... flowing between her and this man who now stood next to her, waiting to help her down.

She glanced at the tall preacher. Did he feel it, too?

No, that was silly. She really should be more sober about things. Not so fanciful. After all, she wasn't a princess in a novel. She was just plain old Lyna Marshall, hired help. She gathered her skirts, studiously avoiding Mr. Marek's eyes as he guided her to the ground. But she couldn't help noticing that she barely came up to his chin. And that his black hair curled slightly at the nape of his neck, just like she had always pictured the dashing Mr. Darcy's hair to be every time she read *Pride and Prejudice*. Not that she would ever picture herself anything like the lovely Elizabeth Bennett, of course. Her own hair was much too reddish for that, anyway, and—

Stop it, Lyna. Pa was always griping about her imagination running away with her. *Maybe you were right, Pa.* One would think she'd never been close to a man before.

****

"Yoo hoo! Preacher! We're over here!"

Andrew, still holding Lyna's hand, turned in the direction of Opal's voice.

What in the world?

He felt his jaw drop as he watched the normally spry Opal come hobbling down the walk, a cane in one hand and the other wrapped in a sling. Armilda followed in a wheelchair, rolling herself at a snail's pace down the walk. Armilda's normally well-kept silver hair looked as if it had gotten caught in a—a tornado. Both women were grinning like they had won a blue ribbon at the Bell County fair.

Andrew had no words. *And was that a...a* dog *in Armilda's lap?* It was a roly-poly little creature with a black face that appeared to have been smooshed up against the wall, and floppy, black, triangular ears. He had never seen anything like it.

"Looks like you found our gal, all right." Opal wobbled to a halt next to him.

She gave Lyna a thorough once-over. "You're prettier than I imagined, young lady." She poked Andrew's foot with her cane tip. "Don't you think so, Preacher?"

Andrew gulped and nodded. Pretty indeed. *But what in heaven's name—*

Armilda wheeled forward. "Welcome to the Daisy Patch, Miss Marshall. Y'all both just come in the house now. We've managed to make some refreshments, even in our condition."

She poked at her hair, managing to make it stick up even more wildly than before, then patted the furry lump that lay panting in her lap. "Oscar, here, has been waiting for you to come too. He needs his bath, and it's sometimes a bit much for Sister and I to manage, you know," she said, her soft voice trembling.

Oscar? Andrew stifled the urge to laugh. *This was ridiculous. What was going on here?* He glanced from Armilda to Opal.

"Now, Miss Opal—"

Miss Opal glared at him just like his teacher had when he missed an answer in Latin class, then motioned at Lyna with her head.

He snapped his mouth closed. He would play along for right now, but once he got Miss Opal by herself…

The old women did an about-face and straggled back up the walkway toward the house, obviously expecting him and Miss Marshall to follow.

Behind him, Lyna started making an odd choking noise.

What now? Was she—?

A giggle escaped, and she held her handkerchief over her mouth, her face red. "I'm—fine." She giggled again. "Why didn't you warn me? I was expecting some shriveled up—"

"And Miss Armilda's hair—" *What had gotten into the Wilson sisters?* Andrew felt helpless against the chuckle rising in his throat, and watching Lyna laugh only made it worse. Finally, he joined her until they were both doubled over next to the wagon.

He recovered first and watched her dab her eyes and fan herself. When had he laughed like that with someone? He couldn't remember.

"We'd best obey, is all I can say." He glanced toward the house where Armilda headed around the side toward the back door, the wheels of the unwieldy chair squeaking with every turn, and little Oscar trotting behind her.

Lyna pulled herself together with a deep breath and nodded. "I must look a mess. My freckles are worse when I've been laughing so hard."

Andrew wanted nothing more at that moment than to examine those freckles up close. The thought shocked him.

"You look lovely," he blurted out, then instantly regretted it. He had no right saying things like that to any other woman than Margaret…and certainly not to a woman he had just met an hour ago.

Lyna shrugged. "That's what my papa always says. I don't believe him, either."

Hmm. Unfortunately, he wouldn't be the one to convince her of it. He was practically a married man.

Chapter Four

Opal peeked out the kitchen window, being careful not to stir the lace curtains as she spied on the couple outside. "She's prettier'n a Texas sunset, Armilda."

Armilda climbed out of the wheelchair and stretched her legs, peering over her sister's shoulder. "Mmmhmm. I just hope she sings as good as she looks."

"And cooks, too." Opal clapped her hand to her mouth and whirled from the window to face her sister. "Lord have mercy, Armilda! We forgot to put that in the newspaper advertisement. What if she can't cook?"

Armilda sniffed. "I know my way around the kitchen, so if she can't, I'll have her turning out baked bean salad and Scottish Fancies in no time."

Opal winced and turned back to the window. "I hope she's a quick study," she murmured, watching the young couple pause by the daisy patch. "We have only three months."

****

"That was a meal fit for a king, Miss Opal." Andrew pushed his chair back slightly. "I imagine it was a little hard to prepare, with your arm injured and all."

He stared hard at Opal.

"Yes, well, it was a bit of a trial," Opal quavered. "But the good Lord helped me through. And you know Armilda is quite a cook herself. She made the dessert." She cast a fond glance at her sister.

Armilda raised her eyebrows at Andrew. "Be a dear and fetch the peach cobbler from the kitchen, would you? It's a little tiresome to maneuver this chair through the door."

Andrew glanced at Lyna, but she didn't seem to detect anything out of the ordinary, though he had caught her looking askance at Miss Armilda's hair as they all sat down to the meal. Of course, she didn't know the sisters like he did, but still…

He shook his head and rose to head for the kitchen, nearly tripping over the pint-sized dog that slept under the table. What was the silly little thing's name? Orville? Oswald? He still couldn't believe Opal and Armilda actually had a dog—and were letting it in the house.

He grabbed the dessert off of the sideboard, then paused at Lyna's soft Texas drawl, so different than Margaret's strident Boston accent.

"I always dreamed about living in a house like this," she said. "It's so grand. It reminds me of the

House Beautiful in *Pilgrim's Progress*. I can just imagine you both there. I think you would be Charity, Miss Armilda. I can tell already. And Miss Opal would be Prudence."

Andrew snickered, picturing Opal's face. Prudence was probably not the most apt description of the old lady. More like precocious. Or persistent. But he had to smile at Miss Marshall's vivid imagination.

He returned, cobbler in hand. "My favorite scene in *Pilgrim's Progress* is when Christian fights Apollyon." He set the dessert on the dining room table. "May I serve you ladies?"

"Yes, please." Lyna turned her smile toward him. "My favorite is when Christian and Hopeful are trapped in the Giant Despair's castle."

Opal scrunched up her face. "Why is that your favorite part, dear?" she asked. "It's so dreary."

"Yes, ma'am," Lyna said. "But I like it because I've been there. Locked in the Giant's castle, I mean."

Andrew raised his eyebrows. How unusual to hear a young woman speak so frankly. "I have, too," he confessed. Rather a lot lately, it seemed.

Lyna glanced around the table. "And then finally, just like Christian, I remembered I had had the key to the door the whole time. All I had to do was use it."

Andrew noticed the glint of tears in Miss Opal's eyes. In her eighty-some years, she had surely faced many such giants. She couldn't have gained so much wisdom otherwise.

She pulled a handkerchief from inside her sling and dabbed delicately at her eyes. "Remind us what the key is, darlin'."

"The key is to remember God's promises, Miss Opal. When we forget His promises, we lose hope and are trapped in the Castle of Doubt. But when we remember His promises, and we thank him for them, that's the key that sets us free from the terrible Giant of Despair."

Armilda beamed at Lyna. "That's some fine preachin' there, Andrew. You might use that in your sermon on Sunday."

"Yes, ma'am." Andrew dug his spoon into his cobbler. He hoped he wouldn't have to say more, because somehow his whole world had shifted since that first gaze into a pair of green eyes a few hours ago. What he would do about that, he didn't know, but there it was. He'd better start praying. Quick.

****

Lyna snuggled into the down mattress, hardly able to believe her good fortune. The Wilsons—and this house—were not what she had expected at all. Though she had been game for an adventure, she had harbored moments of doubt about the whole thing. Last night, her final night at home, she had lain half-awake, imagining herself as a lovely fairy-tale princess, cruelly imprisoned and doomed to hard labor in the wicked lord's dreadful castle. Or rather, the wicked sisters' dreadful castle.

She toiled through the days and nights, her poor knees rough and bleeding from scrubbing the cinder floor; her hands red and calloused beyond repair. And the stream so far away, and the water buckets so heavy. The flaxen-haired young girl stumbled along the rocky path, her frail form bending beneath the weight that was far too heavy for one her age to bear. Oh, how could she smuggle a message to the brave knight? When would he return as promised? She pictured his dark, slightly wavy hair falling over his forehead ... his mysterious brown eyes gazing into the depths of her own—

Oh, wait. That sounded like Mr. Marek. *Andrew*, Miss Opal had called him.

Lyna flopped over onto her back and stared toward the large window. Darkness had fallen an hour ago, and in the blackness, she could see the lights of the fireflies flicking here and there. Was Andrew watching the fireflies, too? He had recently moved from the Wilson's into his own little house down the street, she had learned.

"The poor lonely preacher lives there all by himself," Miss Opal had confided to her after he had left for the evening.

Lyna smiled. If she didn't know better, she would almost think that Miss Opal was trying to match her up with Andrew Marek. But that couldn't be, because she had seen him at the train station just this afternoon, saying goodbye to that other young lady. Surely that woman must be his intended.

But when she did marry, it would be to someone like Mr. Marek. A real circuit-riding preacher. She had thrilled to the stories of her grandfather, the firebrand preacher, Paul Daniels, her entire life. For twenty years, he had labored in God's harvest fields, his bride at his side, preaching God's word and leading many a soul to the cross. Even now, Lyna's heart beat faster at the thought.

"I'm ready to go where you call me, God," she had prayed many times. Her heart yearned to serve God in such a bold way. Yet until today, she had been tied to the ranch.

I need you here more'n God needs you, Lyna, Papa always said. *Besides, you're jest a little slip of a girl.*

That much was true, at least. But what she lacked in height, she made up for in spirit. At least that's what she consoled herself with when she was feeling down. And Mama would have wanted her to follow God, no matter what. Mama, who raised her children with a deep love and reverence for God, even though her own father had banished her from home, knew what she was talking about. It was through those dark days of being alone and pregnant that Mama had truly learned the depths of God's mercy, she had told Lyna many a time. And then she had married Papa.

A good man, Mama always said about him.

He *was* a good man, her papa. If only he could understand her deep drive, her thirst to follow the One who gave His life for her…the depth of her yearning to lead others to salvation in Jesus Christ. But Papa thought it was good enough to go to church whenever the preacher came to town and to say grace over the meal every night.

Lyna drew a deep breath, then let it out slowly, picturing her home, the Bar Three Ranch. Papa always expected her to work as hard as Jacob, but she didn't mind. Those long, quiet hours out on the range provided her plenty of time to dream.

After reading about Amy Carmichael's missionary work in India, she had pictured herself mothering poor, orphan girls in small, mud huts…but then there were people like Hudson Taylor in China, or…or D. L. Moody who had labored right here in America, in Chicago. She had even heard of the "Hallelujah Lassies," seven British women who had helped bring the message of the gospel through the Salvation Army to America in the 1880s. There were so many exciting possibilities. But no matter the version of the dream, always, in her prayerful wonderings, she worked alongside her husband. Just like the stories she had heard of her grandparents. The two of them, in God's service together.

She flipped back over onto her stomach, listening to the sounds of her new world. The sisters' voices still murmuring to one another. Oscar's snuffling at her door. The silky, shushing sounds of oleander branches brushing her window sill. It had been a good day.

****

"Good morning, Miss Opal." Lyna had followed the scent of bacon and the sound of humming to the kitchen, somewhat relieved to have gained a reprieve from cooking for the sisters on her very first day, especially after the supper they served last night. There was no way she could ever hope to prepare something as wonderful as Miss Armilda's pot roast. And worse, the sisters had one of those fancy new electric stoves. She had never even seen one before today. How would she ever tell them that she couldn't cook? Maybe they would send her back to the ranch. Her heart sank, but she could only do her best.

"Shouldn't I be fixing breakfast for you?" she asked.

Opal stopped mid-hum and turned from the stove. "Well, now, we'll have time to talk about all of that later. Today is Women's Wednesday Club." She fidgeted with her sling. "I don't know what's taking Armilda so long, but I—"

"I'm coming along, Sister." Armilda grunted as she manhandled the wheelchair through the doorway. "I seem to be having a little trouble with my skirt, somehow." Her glasses hung precariously on the end of her nose, and she pushed them up to peer through them at Lyna. "Do you know anything about these contraptions, dear?" She gestured to the wheelchair.

Lyna squatted next to the elderly woman, glad to see that Armilda's hair was not quite as wild as it was yesterday. She had to admit, she had wondered a bit about the sisters after meeting them for the first time yesterday. Her face went hot as she recalled her unladylike laughing fit with Andrew. Oh, dear. The man must think her terribly rude. But then again, he had laughed too.

She helped Armilda extricate the hem of her skirt from the wheelchair, then straightened back up. "How long have you been in the chair, Miss Armilda?"

"Oh, well…not too long," Armilda said faintly. "It sure is a doggone nuisance."

It would be rather indelicate to ask what was wrong with the woman, Lyna decided. Maybe when she knew her a little better. "May I fix you a plate?"

"Oh, no. I'm perfectly capable—"

Opal harrumphed.

"I mean, yes, please, dear. I *am* feeling a little weak this morning." Armilda touched her forehead with the back of a limp hand.

Lyna raised her eyebrows. Armilda Wilson looked about as weak as a…as a bulldog. She decided to change the subject. "What does one do at a Wednesday Women's Club?"

Opal whirled around and stared at Lyna. "Why, my dear, have you never been to a Women's Club?"

"No, ma'am." Lyna looked from one sister to the other. "Until I came here, I hardly left the ranch."

"Not even to go to school?"

"No, ma'am. My mama schooled my brother and me."

The two sisters exchanged glances.

"But you're so well-spoken," Opal said.

Lyna shrugged. "Mama was educated back East. Even though we were stuck on the ranch, she wanted us to learn all we could. Papa used to get so angry with her for spending so much money on books and music."

Armilda's voice gentled. "Used to?"

"Mama went to Heaven a year ago. I still miss her dreadfully."

The sisters made sympathetic clucking noises, and Opal gave her a one-armed hug. "Well, we're glad you're here, darlin'. And the Women's Club meeting starts at 9:00, so we'd best be on our way. It's just down the way, at the Central Hotel."

After the trial of getting Armilda settled in the carriage, Lyna climbed up into the tall driver's seat. She might not know how to cook an egg over-easy, but she did know horses. "Just tell me the way," she said over her shoulder.

The two sisters were having a frantic, whispered conversation in the back seat. She could only hear little snatches. "…can't be seen…explain…"

"I think I'll drive us this time, dear." Opal finally leaned up toward Lyna. "We'll drop you off at T.W. Cochran's to fetch the dry goods while we're at the meeting. It will save time."

Save time for what? But after all, the Wilsons were paying her—and paying her well—to do what they needed her to do. She scooted over from the driver's side to make room for Miss Opal to take the reins. "Do you have a list?" she asked.

Armilda cleared her throat. "Just get what you think we'll need for supper for when the preacher comes over tomorrow night before he leaves. He'll be gone for two weeks, so we need to send him off with a good meal."

Lyna gulped. "About cooking supper—"

Miss Opal raised an eyebrow. "What did you cook on the ranch, dear? I'm sure the preacher would love anything you make. He's not a fussbudget."

That was good to know. However, Miss Opal could not possibly fathom the extent of Lyna's cooking failures. She either burnt everything to a crisp or served it woefully underdone, and she never could get the hang of having all of the dishes ready to be served at the same time. "I've not cooked on an electric stove before." She squirmed a little on the hard seat. That was true. But definitely not the whole truth. She clasped her hands together in a knot and turned to face the sisters head on. If they chose to send her back to the ranch, then so be it.

"The truth is that I am a terrible cook." There. She had said it.

"Now, now." Miss Armilda leaned forward to pat her on the shoulder. "If that's all you're worried about, I can teach you. If I could teach Margaret—"

Margaret? Who was Margaret?

Miss Opal coughed loudly. "Armilda will have you whipping up goodies in no time, won't you, Sister?"

"So I may stay?" Until this moment, Lyna hadn't realized how much she had been worrying about the possibility of being asked to leave.

Both women stared at her.

"Stay? Of course you will stay." Miss Opal patted her cheek with her good hand. "Darlin', we've only just begun."

****

Andrew decided to walk the few blocks up Main Street to the Daisy Patch for his supper with the

Wilson's—and Lyna, of course. It would be silly to saddle Moses for that short of a ride, and besides, the glorious sunset beckoned him to linger outside. He ambled down Main Street, greeting his neighbors and admiring the crepe myrtle trees still in bloom. He hadn't done much ambling during Margaret's long visit. Her every waking moment was filled with some sort of activity, and he had been obliged to join in.

He had soon realized that though he enjoyed the busyness of being about his work, he despised busyness for its own sake. He much preferred having time to think. And he had been thinking quite a bit in the quiet moments of these last few days.

He spied Miss Opal on her front porch. Her broom flew as she whisked the front steps.

He grinned to himself as he noticed that she used both hands, with no sling in sight.

She set the broom aside as he moseyed up the walkway and pulled the sling back over her arm, no doubt hoping he hadn't noticed. "I hope you're hungry," she said.

Andrew pecked her cheek. "As a horse."

She smiled at him, then looked at him closer. "What's bothering you, Andrew?"

He shook his head, but she grasped his hand and held on.

How could she always tell when he needed a listening ear? He fidgeted. It would feel awkward to talk to Miss Opal about such things. But then again—

She held his hand tight, waiting.

"How can I possibly marry Margaret, Miss Opal?" He hadn't meant to burst out with it, but there it was.

"Ah, I see." Miss Opal let go of his hand. "Shall we sit, dear?"

He followed her over to the rocking chairs. "I'm stuck, Miss Opal. I—"

She fingered the brooch at her collar. "It's not a sin to break an engagement, Andrew."

"I know. But it's more than that." He stared off into the distance for a moment. He might as well tell her all of it. She'd probably find out somehow anyway, knowing Miss Opal. "I gave my word to her father that I would take care of her. Financially."

Miss Opal frowned and put her glasses on. "I was under the impression that Margaret hailed from a well-to-do family."

"Yes." He rubbed his hand over the back of his neck. "But what she doesn't know is that her father's fortune is running out. Her life of luxury is going to come to an end soon, and her father is trying to minimize the effects of it by having Margaret and her sisters married off by the time it happens."

"I see." She took his hand again and squeezed it. "And you're not quite up to the role of knight in shining armor."

He nodded. And on top of that, a familiar restlessness stirred his spirit. He sensed God preparing his heart for a new task. He wasn't sure what yet, but he could feel the yearning in his spirit … the unrelenting pull to be about His Father's work in an untried field … a fresh calling of sorts. He had recently read one of Charles Spurgeon's sermons, and one particular point had stuck in his mind. *Let the purpose of God, for which you ought to adore Him every day, be plenteously fulfilled in you, and let it be seen that He has chosen you to know Christ that you may make Him known to others!*

So there it was, in a nutshell. All he knew for sure was that God had called him to Texas for a reason—to make Christ known to as many as possible. And that life with Margaret didn't seem to fit the picture.

"What's the good Lord saying to you?" Opal peered at him through her glasses, her eyes magnified eyes serious.

He winced. "I'm not clear about that yet, Miss Opal."

"Well, you know by now that you've got to do more than pray. You have to listen, too, darlin'." She hefted herself out of the rocker. "I'll be praying."

That's what he was afraid of. Because when Miss Opal prayed, things happened. He leaned his head back and closed his eyes as she disappeared into the house.

The rocker squeaked on the floorboards as he lingered a few more minutes. His thoughts drifted to

Lyna. He couldn't deny the attraction he felt for her. She was everything Margaret was not. She was soft-spoken. She was intelligent. She was—

She was singing. His eyes popped open as she came around the side of the house from the back door and headed toward the daisy patch, a basket in her hands.

He sat transfixed. He had never heard such a melodic voice. But it was more than that. Beyond the exquisite sound, he sensed a depth of emotion—as if she were pouring her whole being into the words:

> My Jesus, I love thee, I know thou art mine.
> For thee all the folly of sin I resign.
> My gracious Redeemer, my Savior art thou,
> If ever I loved thee, my Jesus 'tis now.

He turned away then, not wanting to intrude upon her privacy. But something had happened. Her sweet spirit, revealed so clearly, had opened a door in his heart that he hadn't known was closed.

****

He pondered this as he sat across from her at the Wilson's dining room table, admiring her. Lovely inside and out. And that dimple in her right cheek was adorable. "I hear that you were our chef tonight, Miss Marshall."

She flushed and glanced at Miss Armilda. "I'm afraid I did little more than help Miss Armilda. I'm not a very good—"

"She made the rolls all by herself with her special recipe from the ranch." Miss Opal beamed at him as she passed him the bread basket. "Looks like you haven't tried one yet."

Andrew eyed the pale flat things in the basket. They looked more like hard-tack than rolls, but all of the women were staring at him, so he took two. Maybe he could smuggle them into his pocket when no one was watching. Or perhaps Oscar would enjoy one in lieu of a bone.

In the end, he had slathered them with butter and used them to scoop up the rest of the gravy on his plate. A little crunchy, but sometime during supper he had discovered that he was quite hesitant to do anything that would make that dimple disappear.

****

Andrew threw his saddlebag onto the bunk at Bascom Tulley's ranch. He had already been on the road for a week and half, and he could feel the weariness in his body and his spirit. At least Bascom and his wife always welcomed him heartily whenever he came to supply the Sparks church. It couldn't really be called a church—more of a meeting out under the live oaks on Bascom's land. There wasn't much out here this far southeast of Temple and Belton except cotton fields and cattle ranches. But the people were hard-working, honest folks. Folks who needed marrying and burying and everything in between. But mostly they needed the Word of God preached to them.

Bascom appeared at the bunkhouse door, his weathered face lit up with a grin. "Come on up to the house, Preacher. Martha's got some fine pheasant in the oven."

Andrew's stomach growled as he and Bascom crossed the field.

"You're lookin' a little down in the mouth today." The old rancher reached out to push the gate open.

Did it show that much?

"Sometimes I wonder why God chose me to do this." Andrew kicked at a rock, and cloud of dust swirled up.

Bascom always lent a listening ear. When Andrew had first moved down here to Texas, the fire burning in his soul to spread God's Word in the West had consumed him. He had grown weary of the pomp and circumstance of the churches back in Boston and longed to share the pure gospel with those in need. But people were people, he was discovering, no matter where one lived.

"I guess I'm just discouraged, Bascom. Last week I rode for four hours and only two families showed up for service."

His friend nodded.

"The time before that, it poured rain all weekend, and no one offered a place to hold the meeting. I might as well have not even bothered." He fell silent, thinking of the many hours he had spent traveling around to the different ranches and farms, helping to haul in crops, rebuild after the tornado, sit up all night with an invalid…all in God's name. He longed for these people to see the love of Christ in him so they would hear him when he talked about the hope found in God's Word. But his heart was broken time and again when he would pass a saloon and find one of his ranch-hand friends lying in the dust outside, stone drunk.

"The way I see it, the good Lord tol' ya to go, and you're a-goin'." Bascom spit on the ground. "It's his business if folks don't want to hear it."

****

Andrew lay in his bunk that night, thinking about Bascom's words. Sometimes he needed to be reminded that it was God's work and not a preacher's striving that brought change to sinners' hearts. But God worked through his servants, too. And he, Andrew Marek, was such a weak vessel for God to use. He groaned out loud. Occasionally, Miss Opal had to preach him one of her sermons, and that always set him back on track. Come to think of it, he could use one of those right now.

"It's not by might, nor by power, but by my Spirit, says the Lord." He quoted her favorite scripture out loud, picturing her pointing to it right there in the book of Zechariah. He felt a little better. And folks *were* grateful for his services, though sometimes it seemed that that's all folks wanted from him—funerals and weddings. Some aspired to more than that, for sure. Particularly the women who constantly tried to marry their daughters off to him.

He grimaced. Why any mother would want their daughter to marry him was beyond his understanding. This life would be hard for any woman. She would need to either travel around with him, or be willing for him to be gone for long stretches of time, leaving her alone. And she would be expected to wear all kinds of hats—from song leader to nurse to counselor to cook to Bible teacher.

He stared out the window at the unending prairie, and once again had a hard time imagining Margaret being willing to live this life alongside of him. She had long professed her love for him, even when as children their families lived next door to each other. He still had a vivid recollection of the time their families had vacationed together at the beach. He was fifteen, and Margaret was fourteen. Out on the boardwalk, surrounded by throngs of beachgoers, he managed to kiss her on the cheek without either of their fathers noticing.

But Margaret had changed and so had he. He rolled his head to stretch the kinks out of his neck. He felt stuck. Trapped.

A pair of green eyes and a soft Texas drawl flashed into his mind. Lyna Marshall might be diminutive in size, but the few glimpses he had gotten of her spirit revealed depth and substance. Her keen intelligence and obvious love for God delighted him.

He remembered her tanned skin, the roughness of her hand when he had clasped it for just a moment, and knew she was no stranger to hard work. He had glimpsed the sorrow in her eyes when she spoke of her mother, had sensed the bubbling joy in her spirit when she giggled out loud. She was part of this country called Texas. She lived close to the earth and the seasons like every one that made up his little congregations in these outlying areas. She would understand the heartbreak of a failed crop, the desperation of watching a loved one die, the simple beauties of living next to the land—a new calf…a rainbow…the music of a brook. How he knew that about her, he couldn't be sure. But the memory of the moment they had laughed together that first day had been like tonic to his spirit.

And her singing had literally taken his breath away the other night. He replayed the moment again.

She hadn't known he was there on the front porch, listening to her sweet voice as she cut yellow daisies for the dining room table. Something had stirred in his heart that night, something that left him with a longing…a sweet but powerful ache that he had never felt before. A feeling that he was somehow missing something…or someone…that he never before realized he wanted or needed.

He yearned to saddle up and fly back to Belton right now. To see if his feelings were real. To look for answers in those eyes. To hold her tight against his heart.

But he had given his word to Margaret and to her father. How could he go back on his promise?

Chapter Five

Opal woke with a start, urgency pressing upon her spirit. She rose and shuffled to her sister's bedroom with only shafts of moonlight to guide her.

"Armilda. Armilda, wake up," she hissed. "We've got to pray for the preacher."

The moon shone high in the sky, and the muggy evening air was still. Not even a hint of a breeze stirred the bedroom drapery. The owl that lived in the cedar tree hooted once, then once more.

Armilda opened one eye. "I've *been* praying for him, Sister."

"No, I mean right now. The good Lord's been talking to me, and we must pray now."

Armilda pushed the quilt aside and slid down stiffly onto her knees beside her sister. "I sure hope he appreciates this."

The sisters joined hands and lifted Andrew before the throne. For long moments, they interceded. Opal was barely aware of the ache in her knees as the presence of the Holy Spirit filled her consciousness, guiding her very thoughts and words. Armilda's hot tears splashed onto Opal's hand as time passed unheeded.

Finally, Opal shifted with a sigh. "It's done."

The weight had lifted.

"Thanks be to God." Armilda blotted her eyes. "Thanks be to God."

****

Andrew was beat. After preaching twice on Sunday, marrying the Peters' girl to Bubby Olsen on Monday and helping Bascom dig a ditch on his ranch on Tuesday, these last two days had finally worn him out. The three-hour horseback ride back to Belton would almost be a relief. At least he could relax when he was in the saddle. Usually. Usually he would sing hymns as Moses trotted along. Sometimes he would preach next week's sermon, just to try it out.

But this time, he had gotten a late start home. He always tried to time it so he would arrive home before dark, but he couldn't leave Bascom in the lurch. Some of Bascom's ranch hands had not returned after the weekend, and the man had a ranch to run. Andrew could have spent the night and headed to Belton in the morning, but after a week, he was anxious for home. And for the sight of a certain auburn-haired woman, if he were honest with himself.

Now, as he and Moses began the journey home in the twilight, the sight of two newly-erected saloons troubled him. Worse was the number of horses and wagons tied up in front of the slovenly establishments. Far too many. Too many men that should have been home with their wives and children.

With a heavy heart, he recognized the horses of some of the very men who had attended his church service on Sunday. Many a good man had lost his family and his self-respect to the demon rum. There must be something that could be done. More and more often, even in Belton, men staggered through the streets in a drunken fog, sometimes even in the middle of the day. This should not be. Those men turned to alcohol instead of to the cross of Jesus Christ. *God, what would you have me do?*

He had recently read about an organization called the Salvation Army. It seemed to have begun in England, but apparently, an Italian Naval Captain named Adam Janelli had established the Salvation Army of Texas in Dallas in the last few years. The way Andrew heard tell, many people had found Christ and freedom from alcohol. If God could use a layman like that, He could sure use—

Moses flicked his head hard, jerking the reins from Andrew's hands. This horse could be so temperamental sometimes.

"What is it, boy?" Andrew regained the reins.

The horse swung his head over and up, almost as though he wanted to see his master on his back. The animal seemed agitated. Maybe something was rubbing or poking him.

By now, they were well out of town and well on the way to Belton, and though he usually felt relatively safe, it was pretty lonely country out here.

And not much of a road, either. He'd traveled it enough that he knew he wouldn't get lost, but he still didn't care to linger in the open prairie with dusk coming on.

He slid off the horse, then ran his hand under the sweaty saddle. Nothing. He chugged some lukewarm water from his canteen. The poor beast probably felt as weary and irritable as he did. But they had only a little more than an hour to go and they would be home. Before he had left last week, Miss Opal, her keen blue eyes fixed on him, had made him promise to be back in time for the hymn sing.

"Miss Marshall will be playing the piano," she had announced. And then, "It's a wonder that girl isn't married yet."

He shook his head as he climbed back up into the saddle. Miss Opal was about as subtle as a rancher lassoing a calf. Apparently, she and Miss Armilda didn't quite approve of Margaret being his wife. But they didn't—

Moses would not budge. He had locked his four black legs into place and stood stalwartly, his nostrils flaring.

"What's wrong with you, Mo?" Andrew gently nudged the horse to no avail. "We're headed home, boy. Don't you want to be back in your own stable?" How ridiculous trying to reason with an animal, but he'd never been good with horses and this one could be particularly obstinate at times. He'd gotten the creature from one of the ranchers out in Little River when he first moved down here from Boston. The man assured him the young horse was "broke in real good." Ha.

Andrew dug his heels in again, then stopped, feeling sweat prickle in his armpits. He was being watched. But by whom? And why? It was almost fully dark now, but the moon hung high and bright in the inky sky. From the road—if one could call it that—Andrew could still make out the scrubby mesquite and prairie grass, rippling in the never-ending wind. Not much place for someone to hide. The Biblical story of Balaam and the donkey from the Bible flitted across his mind.

God, are you trying to give me a message, and I'm not listening? Or is someone waiting to harm me?

He scanned the prairie and spoke aloud. "'He that dwelleth in the secret place of the Most High shall abide under the shadow of the Almighty. I will say of the LORD, He is my refuge and my fortress: my God; in him will I trust.'" Perhaps whoever hid out there needed to hear it as much as he did.

He raised his voice louder. "'Surely he shall deliver thee from the snare of the fowler, and from the noisome pestilence.'" He patted the side of Moses' neck, and the horse relaxed his rigid stance. *God, I pray for your protection right now. Hide me under the shadow of your wings. Send your angels to guard me, I pray.*

"'He shall cover thee with his feathers, and under his wings shalt thou trust: his truth shall be thy shield and buckler'" Faith swelled in his heart. He nudged the horse with his toe, and Moses walked slowly, as if waking from a trance. "'Thou shalt not be afraid for the terror by night; nor for the arrow that flieth by day…'"

Without warning, Moses broke into a wild gallop.

Andrew reached for his pistol, while still loudly reciting Psalm 91. From behind him, a bullet whizzed past his ear, then another. It would be folly to waste time trying to turn around to see if he could spot anyone.

"Come on, Moses." He urged the horse with his heels. "God! Help me!"

A barrage of bullets flew at him from both sides of the road now, but it seemed as if an invisible shield protected him. Moses shrieked and galloped on.

Andrew held his pistol in one hand and the reins in the other. He would shoot if he had to, but every cell in his body rebelled at the thought.

Moses veered off the dirt road and onto the narrow path that dipped down near Little River, then pounded over the bridge, back up onto the main road.

Only a few more miles.

He glanced over his shoulder.

No one behind him.

Thank God. He urged Moses on another mile.

The old Little River fort ruins had to be near. Many a Texas Ranger and frontier settler had taken refuge here from the Indians in years gone by. Now, the aging timber structure was just a shell, but he knew a spring ran nearby.

Moses wouldn't hold out much longer at this pace.

He glanced behind him again. Still no one in sight.

Moments later, he pulled Moses to a stop near the fort and slid off the horse. He ran a shaking hand across his eyes. God had surely spared his life. He had had a couple of other close calls before, but nothing like this. Why would someone shoot at him? If they had meant to rob him, that probably could have been easily accomplished while he stood near the mesquite thicket checking Moses' saddle. And besides, he didn't exactly look like a prosperous traveler.

On top of that, most folks around here knew him. Or at least knew that he was the preacher. He couldn't think of one person who would have a vendetta against him. Maybe some unsavory characters were just passing through the area. Holdups did happen occasionally, particularly since the train tracks weren't far from here.

He led Moses to the spring, and they both drank deeply. Cool water after a sweltering Texas day became a blessing in and of itself. Andrew flopped down in the tall grass, his heart rate finally returning back to normal. If he had to guess, there had been an entire army of angels surrounding him and Moses back there on the road. Now that he thought about it, he recalled that only a few weeks ago a traveling salesman had been robbed and beaten in that very spot. How could he have forgotten? He had just been so disturbed about the saloons that he hadn't paid attention as well as usual. Yet another reason to despise the scourge of liquor. The same kind of men who would frequent a saloon were the same rough characters who would rob and kill.

After a few minutes of rest, he climbed back into the saddle. The powdery dust stuck to his sweaty skin, and he just wanted to crawl into his bunk. Thank God home lay just up ahead. Had he missed the hymn sing? No, that was tomorrow night. He couldn't wait to share with Lyna—to share with the others—how God had protected him tonight. Not to mention that he had promised Miss Opal he would be there. And a promise to Miss Opal was not something to take lightly.

Chapter Six

Opal fastened the brooch onto her collar, then checked her reflection in the mirror. She had worn this same brooch every day of her life now for almost sixty years, but recently, the sight of it caused her to long for heaven a little more than usual.

The sweet sound of Lyna's voice, lifted in song, reached her ears, and she smiled. The good Lord still had work for this eighty-one-year-old woman to do on this earth. She mustn't be pining for what could have been.

She turned as she heard Armilda slip into the room. "This is no ordinary young woman God has sent us, Sister," she said.

Armilda nodded. "Yes, ma'am. Do you think the preacher is ready?"

Opal pictured Andrew's dear face. Both she and Armilda had come to love this earnest young man like a son. "I don't know, but the good Lord's been talking to me again. It's time to begin the next part of the plan. I will post the letter to Margaret in the morning."

"But what about church on Sunday morning?" Armilda sank onto the side of the bed. "I don't relish trying to explain—"

It *was* rather a dreadful thought. As pillars of the community, she and Armilda had a reputation to uphold. Neither of them had ever ventured out of their home with as much as one hair out of place. And now the entire church would be privy to—

She sighed. "It's a cross that must be borne, Sister."

"And to think she called you Prudence," Armilda muttered.

****

Lyna followed Miss Opal out the back door, pushing Miss Armilda's chair. The morning air was less hot than usual, so they had decided to walk the few blocks to church.

"I'm so thrilled to attend church with you two this morning. At home, everybody meets under the big oak by the river for church meetings." She stopped the wheelchair by the daisy patch for a moment to disentangle Miss Armilda's skirt from one of the wheels. "We only have services about once a month or whenever the preacher comes."

"Is he as fine a preacher as our Andrew?" Miss Opal raised her eyebrows.

Lyna laughed at the elderly woman's fierce tone. "I've never heard Rev. Marek preach, Miss Opal. But I'd love to." She bent to pick a daisy, hoping to hide her flaming face. She shouldn't be thinking about

Andrew in that way because he was already spoken for. Wasn't he? She hadn't yet been bold enough to ask about the young woman at the train depot. Or maybe she didn't want to know the answer.

The sisters glanced at each other.

"Well, you're sure to hear a timely word from the good Lord today, dear," Miss Armilda said as Lyna pushed her down the walkway. "Our Reverend Townsend is a well-spoken man."

"He's a professor at Baylor Female College, too." Opal beamed. "Of course, he wasn't there when Armilda and I taught there. He's too young."

Lyna stopped. "You taught at the college? Both of you?"

"Yes, ma'am." Miss Opal waved her cane in the general vicinity of the church. "We've been part of this community for as long as we can remember."

No wonder the woman on the train had said everyone in Belton knew the Wilson sisters.

"We've been members of First Baptist Church of Belton since it was founded 54 years ago. Our papa and mama, too. Until they passed, of course." Armilda looked up at her sister. "Opal's been the church teller since the very first day."

Lyna pondered this as they strolled the few blocks to the large brick building she had noticed when Andrew first brought her to the Wilsons'. She admired it now as they neared. A grand building, it had two steeples and five arched, stained-glass windows on each side. Several more windows graced the front, and she could hardly wait to see what it looked like inside. She had only dreamed about worshipping in a such a place.

She heard Miss Armilda take a deep breath as they approached the door.

"Why, Miss Armilda. Have you taken ill?" An older gentleman held the church door wide enough for Lyna to push the wheelchair through.

"Oh, it's nothing to be concerned about, Mr. Edwards. But thank you for your concern." Miss Armilda brushed him off, motioning for Lyna to keep pushing.

Miss Opal marched next to them, keeping her gaze straight ahead. Lyna had never seen her look so stern. Perhaps her arm pained her more than she let on. Lyna gave the older woman a quick hug as they settled in a pew.

Lyna sensed an excited hum in the air, and guessed that it must surround the sisters' somewhat frazzled appearance, though she had taken pains to style their hair this morning as directed. Their health issues must have been a recent turn of events, she decided. Maybe that's when they had placed the advertisement in the newspaper.

But what had happened to the sisters for them both to be injured at once? Maybe their wagon had overturned somehow. Or … or maybe there had been a tornado. She scrunched up her eyes. Hmm. She couldn't remember hearing about one lately. So... maybe Armilda had been out in back gathering eggs, and an intruder forced his way into the hen house and Miss Opal—no, that didn't sound quite right. She sighed. She'd have to ask them about it sometime, now that she knew them a little better.

The pianist struck a chord, and everyone rose from their wooden pews. Everyone except Miss Armilda in her wheelchair. The organ boomed out grandly as a robed choir filed in.

So intent on the sisters' maladies, Lyna had barely taken in her surroundings until now. The sun streamed through the stained glass windows at the front, splashing rainbows upon the choir members. The sheer beauty of it stole her breath.

She hadn't had much opportunity to attend a service in a real church building. And certainly never one as large as this. Five hundred and seventy-one people, Miss Opal had told her proudly as they strolled to church this morning.

And now when all five hundred and seventy-two raised their voices in song together, a lump rose in Lyna's throat. This glorious sound of many voices praising God together—this surely must be the sound of heaven. Mama sang her beloved hymns up there now, joining with millions of others in worship to the King.

Lyna brushed a tear from her eye, then settled down with everyone else to hear the message from

Rev. E. G. Townsend, the church's full-time pastor. As Miss Armilda had promised, Rev. Townsend spoke eloquently. He urged the congregation to strengthen their faith in God's Word, then ended with a quote from Martin Luther, "Faith is the 'yes' of the heart, a conviction on which one stakes one's life."

That's how it had always been in Lyna's life. Even as a young child, thrilling to the stories of Daniel in the lions' den…Elijah and the prophets of Baal…her heart had always said "yes" to God. *Yes, I will love you. Yes, I will follow you. Yes, I will serve you.* Most of the time, that had been pretty easy. Losing Mama had been hard, but even then, Lyna had not lost her faith in a loving God.

And when she had prayed about coming to Belton, she knew God had provided this opportunity. So here she was. But for what reason? So far, it had been a delightful time of meeting new people and expanding her horizons. But there must be a deeper purpose. *God, what are you saying to me? Where are you leading me?* She had only been at the Wilson's for two weeks and somehow, she knew she would not be going back to the ranch at the end of these three months. God had something for her here. What He had planned, she didn't know. But she would say yes.

****

Up before dawn on laundry day, Lyna filled the huge kettles with water and hefted them onto the stove. While the water heated, she grated soap off of the big chunk in the pantry. At least the sisters had a hand-crank washing machine instead of just a washboard. Still, the laundry would take all day, between washing, wringing, hanging it out to dry, and then ironing. She dreaded the ironing the most. But the washing wasn't too bad, except that it made one's arm so tired.

She poured several buckets of hot water into the clothes-filled drum, added a bit of soap and cranked the handle. The sound of the clothes sloshing around inside made her think of the time she and Jacob had traveled to Galveston Beach with their grandparents. The ocean waves were swishing and swirling around her feet—

The floor creaked, and she glanced toward the dim hallway. She hoped she hadn't wakened the sisters before their usual time. "Good morning?"

No answer.

Odd. She thought she had caught a glimpse of Miss Armilda's head disappearing back into her bedroom. But Miss Armilda couldn't get around without her chair, and anyone could hear the squeaky thing coming from a mile away. It must have been Miss Opal. But it would be pretty hard to mix up the sisters. Miss Opal's short figure had more padding, and she wore her glasses suspended on a chain around her neck. Miss Armilda was taller and more angular …at least she looked as though she'd be taller if she were standing instead of always sitting and she always wore her glasses.

Shrugging, Lyna went back to sloshing and returned to the beach.

Miss Opal appeared an hour later, carrying Oscar in her good arm.

"I think you need to wash this little dog along with the laundry, Lyna." She wrinkled her nose. "He's rather odiferous."

Lyna eyed the panting creature. "Maybe he got into something outside."

Miss Opal opened the back door and deposited the dog on the back porch. "Well, he can stay out there until he is bathed," she said. "Now then, young lady, we need to discuss your piano-playing abilities. It's almost time for the hymn sing and I can't play with my arm in this contraption."

****

With a flourish, Lyna finished playing "How Firm a Foundation." The dozen or so people gathered in the Wilson's parlor murmured their appreciation, and she smiled. She might not be comfortable in the kitchen, but she could play the piano to beat the band, as Papa always said.

Miss Armilda edged her bulky chair up closer to the piano. "How about 'Savior Like a Shepherd Lead Us,' dear?"

Lyna smiled and nodded, not quite sure how she had adjusted from her quiet life on the ranch to playing for a crowded room in Belton in the span of a few of weeks. But here she was on a Wednesday night, thumping away on the stately Chickering grand in the Wilsons' parlor and loving every minute of it. She had learned to play on Mama's old piano at home, learning how to compensate for the high C and the low G keys that always stuck, as well as the missing damper pedal.

Clearly, the Wilson's piano was much finer, with ornate designs caved into its shining cherry-wood. And none of the keys stuck. The first time she had played it, she couldn't believe how much more grand her playing sounded than it had in their small parlor at home. Almost like the pianist she had heard play at church on Sunday.

"Lyna?" Miss Armilda peered at her. "Do you know 'Savior, Like a Shepherd Lead Us'?"

Lyna snapped back to the present.

"That's one of my favorites, Miss Armilda." She didn't even need the hymnal for that one.

She loved to sing it out loud when she rode the range with Jacob, her brother. He would harmonize, and she would picture the Good Shepherd himself, walking over the prairie fields of the Bar Three

Ranch, lovingly carrying a little lamb in his arms. Much like Papa had often carried a sick or injured calf to the barn.

They sang it through, all four verses, and wave of homesickness swept over her. She'd never been away from the ranch for so long. How were Pa and Jacob doing without her?

"Could we sing 'O God Our Help in Ages Past,' Lyna?" Miss Opal called out.

Lyna flipped to the page in the hymnal. Apparently, Miss Opal wasn't the only one who loved the song, because soon the dozen people present were enthusiastically, if not quite harmoniously, belting out the first verse, nearly drowning out the piano.

O God, our help in ages past,
our hope for years to come,
our shelter from the stormy blast,
and our eternal home.

She drew a breath to begin the second verse when behind her, she heard a deep voice join in with the others.

Under the shadow of thy throne,
still may we dwell secure;
sufficient is thine arm alone,
and our defense is sure.

Her fingers faltered on the keys.

Was that Andrew Marek?

She dared not turn around, but she felt sure it had to be the handsome preacher.

She played the last chords of the song and spun slightly on the piano stool to confirm her suspicions. It *was* Andrew. And the poor man looked like he hadn't slept in a week.

****

Andrew met Lyna's welcoming gaze. He had counted the hours until he would see her again. And now, she looked—

"Glad you could join us, Preacher!" One of the other men slapped him on the back. "Just getting back into town?"

"Late last night." He smiled at Lyna. "May I make a request?"

"I'll do my best!"

His pulse rate kicked up when she returned his smile.

"How about 'A Mighty Fortress Is Our God?'" After his narrow escape last night, the song held more meaning than ever.

She nodded. "I can play that one without—"

Miss Opal beamed at both of them. "Oh, I love that one." She clasped Lyna's shoulders. "And you play so beautifully, dear."

Miss Armilda sniffed. "That song makes me think of our dear saintly mother, Sister." She trailed her fingers down the side of the piano. "I remember her playing it many a time on this very piano that Papa had bought for her when they married."

"Yes, I always loved the story of how they met. Papa heard her playing at church one day and fell head over heels in love with her before he ever even knew her name." Opal heaved a rapturous sigh, her hand on her neckline. "God works in mysterious ways, doesn't he, Preacher?"

"Yes, ma'am." He patted her shoulder. "In fact, after we sing, I think we should all join in prayer for you and Miss Armilda. You have both had so many ailments lately."

Sympathetic murmurs of agreement met his suggestion as he caught Lyna's eye. Had she caught on to their little game yet?

"Why, that's so thoughtful of you, Andrew." Miss Opal smiled at him brightly. "And please pray for little Oscar. He was so anxious about his bath that he ran off, and we haven't been able to locate him."

Andrew snorted. Miss Opal, of course, knew that little comment would get his goat. He might as well just give up now.

He rolled his head, trying to relax his shoulders. Last night's drama was taking its toll, and the letter he had received from Margaret this morning had just about finished him off. She more or less informed him that she didn't care to marry him if he wouldn't come back to Boston, and demanded that he do so. Immediately. How he had ever fancied himself in love with her was beyond him. But the problem of what to do about it—her—lingered like the dry unpleasantness of a mouthful of chokecherries.

****

After the singing, Lyna bustled back and forth from the kitchen to the parlor, pouring tea and serving pie. Several days ago, the Wilsons' neighbor, Harriet Nelson, had brought over a peck of peaches, fresh-picked from her two enormous trees. Armilda had parked her chair at the kitchen table and gone straight to work. As she peeled and chopped, she instructed Lyna in the fine art of pie-crust making.

"Don't roll it too thin, mind you." Armilda inspected Lyna's work. "No one likes a pie crust that's too thick or too thin."

Lyna diligently rolled the dough into what was supposed to be a circle, but ended up more like a lopsided rectangle. Then when she tried to fit it into the tin, she ended up having to cut and patch and squish to make it look even remotely like Armilda's perfect crust.

Armilda peered at it over the top of her glasses. "It's not very pretty, Lyna, but the menfolk won't mind. They only care that it tastes good, you know."

Lyna nodded. Why hadn't Mama taught her how to do this? About the only thing Mama had taught her how to bake was everyday salt-rise bread. Or yeast bread, when they could get yeast. "Now we just dump in the peaches and the sugar?"

"No, ma'am. First we mix the peaches together in a bowl with the sugar and cinnamon, then we distribute the peaches equally between both pie tins."

Lyna observed Miss Armilda carefully as the older woman rolled out the dough for the top of the pies. Though Miss Armilda's speech and mannerism spoke of money and a proper upbringing, her hands were work-worn and strong. The streaks of black running through her silvery hair belied her years, and her rose-leaf complexion was still mostly unlined. Sometimes Lyna wondered if Armilda weren't healthier than she let on. But what reason would there be for the woman to be untruthful about her situation?

Maybe she was secretly a princess...born to rule over some far-away land, but she was kidnapped by a cruel uncle and...and forced to travel to Texas with her older, more precocious sister, to...to....

No, that didn't make sense. Maybe, once upon a time, she had married a very, very rich man and—

Lyna's eyes widened. Had Miss Opal or Miss Armilda *ever* been married? She'd never heard either of them mention a husband. Or children, come to think of it.

Armilda draped the top crust over the top of the mounded peaches. "Now we just pinch the top and bottom layers of pie dough together so they'll seal together nicely. You don't want any hot peach juice to bubble out while it's baking. Makes a dadblamed mess in the oven, for one thing."

Lyna pinched and poked her pie dough into submission, but the edges were uneven and lumpy. She frowned at it. "How do you make that pretty edge like the one on the cherry pie you served the other day, Miss Armilda?"

Armilda flushed. "Oh, that?" she said. "It's my own little secret. But I'll show you a good way. You just pinch a little piece of the dough together with your thumb and forefinger, then you poke it in with the forefinger of your other hand. See?"

She worked her way halfway around Lyna's pie, then shoved it across the table for Lyna to try.

****

The result was less than lovely, Lyna thought now as she cut juicy slices for everyone who had stayed after the hymn sing. She helped Armilda arrange them nicely on the "company" china dishes.

When she reentered the parlor, she spotted Andrew Marek slouched on the settee, looking like he could fall asleep any moment. Her stomach did a weird little fluttery thing when he glanced her direction.

"Would you care for a piece of pie, Mr. Marek?" She balanced a dish in each hand.

"Yes, ma'am." He sat up straighter and smiled up at her. "I never met a pie I didn't like."

"Well, you've never met mine," she murmured. And there was a first time for everything, Mama had always said.

Just then, the large piece slid neatly off of Miss Opal's best china plate and onto Andrew's lap. And looking back on the incident later, Lyna was certain this was no accident, but a providential occurrence.

Andrew jumped to catch the pie, but it was too late. It landed in a large, gooey mess on his Sunday-best pants. "I've never had pie served to me in exactly this fashion, Miss Marshall," he said with a straight face.

Lyna grimaced, not quite meeting his eye. Somehow, she knew she would see a twinkle there, and she already knew what would happen next. She would start laughing, and she wouldn't be able to stop. As it was, she could barely contain the giggle bubbling up into her throat. She scurried to the kitchen for a washrag. Maybe if she didn't look at him—

"Ah, Miss Marshall?"

She glanced over her shoulder, and the giggle escaped. She clapped her hand over her mouth. *Stop it, Lyna!* The poor man was cupping his hand over his leg, trying to contain the juice before it made its way to the parlor carpet and here she was, giggling like a ninny.

Fortunately, no one else appeared to have noticed. Miss Opal held court in the opposite end of the parlor near the fireplace, while Miss Armilda and Rev. Townsend's wife discussed a new knitting pattern.

Lyna gathered herself together and handed Andrew a wet cloth. She held a plate near his leg, so he could scrape the worst of it off onto the plate.

"I'm so sorry, Mr. Marek." She took the rag from him. "I don't usually go around dumping people's desserts on their laps, I can assure you."

"Oh, so I'm special, then." He grinned at her.

Her heart flipped over. Yes. Yes, he was.

"Yes." She waved the rag in the air. "I reserved that little trick just for you. Just to liven things up a little bit, since you looked so tired."

He laughed. "Well, your plan worked. I'm certainly more awake than a moment ago. Ah, do you mind if I just serve myself a piece from the kitchen?"

She shook her head. "I don't think Miss Opal would think it proper for a guest to serve himself." She darted a glance in the direction of Miss Opal's group by the fireplace.

"Lyna—I mean, Miss Marshall, I'm hardly a guest. I practically live here when I'm not on the road, if you hadn't noticed."

Yes, she had noticed, actually. And she had also noticed the reddening of his ears when he had slipped and called her by her given name a second ago.

"I wouldn't mind if you called me Lyna." Had she really said that out loud?

He rose and followed her into the sweltering kitchen, where he stood quite close to her near the sideboard.

"I would like that," he said, his voice low. "But you must call me Andrew, then."

Lyna fanned herself. Had the kitchen gotten warmer, or was it just her? She smiled up at him. "Preacher Andrew it is." She laid her hand gently on his cheek for a moment. He was such a dear man. And he looked so very weary.

He covered her hand with his own larger one. "You better be careful, Lyna. Your heart shows in your eyes."

Chapter Seven

Opal had not missed the preacher following Lyna into the kitchen earlier in the evening, nor both of their rosy faces when they came back out. If she wasn't so old, she would dance a little hallelujah dance. Instead, she sashayed into Armilda's room, where she found her sister doing her nightly knee bends. "The plan is working, Sister."

Armilda harrumphed. "Well, I fervently hope so. My backside's never been so flat from sitting in this dadgum chair all day."

"The chair was your idea, if I recall correctly," Opal said, not unkindly. "And according to my best calculations, we should be able to wrap this up in a fortnight or so."

"Law, Opal!" Armilda burst out. "I can't stand this much longer. I'm just going to waltz out into the kitchen tomorrow morning and tell that girl I've had a miraculous healing."

"Now, Sister—"

"The preacher prayed for us to be healed, now, didn't he?"

"Well, yes, but—"

"Your faith is faltering, Opal Wilson. If the good Lord can heal me, then surely he can heal you, too. A *double* miracle!"

Opal grasped her cane. "I'd appreciate it if you would just stick to the plan, Armilda."

"Just a deplorable lack of faith, I'm telling you," Armilda grumbled. "That's all it is, plain and simple."

****

Lyna could hardly wait. After breakfast was cleared and the morning chores completed, she would finally have a chance to visit the library. Every time they had driven past the building, she shivered at the treasures that must lie behind those ornate doors.

"How long has the library been there?" Lyna poured coffee for both of the sisters.

"Two years." Miss Opal passed the fruit bowl to her sister. "The Wednesday Women's Club donated the first 1,000 books to the library."

"Mostly classics, of course." Miss Armilda sipped her coffee.

Miss Opal nodded. "None of those new novels that would just put garbage in one's head, you know." She shuddered. "I can hardly get over all of the hullabaloo about that *Call of the Wild* book."

Lyna was slightly disappointed in this, since she was quite partial to novels, particularly ones that had beautiful heroines and dramatic endings. Speaking of which—

She placed the plate of hot biscuits on the table before she spoke, taking care not to repeat the food-sliding-off-the-plate disaster of the other evening. Her biscuits still didn't look exactly like the ones Miss Armilda had served the other morning, but at least they weren't burnt this time.

"Miss Opal, I've been meaning to ask you who that young woman was with Andr—I mean Rev. Marek—the day I arrived in Temple."

She had lain awake long into the night after the pie incident, reliving her kitchen conversation with Andrew. Was it possible that he was interested in her as more than just the Wilson's hired help? The look in his eye almost led her to believe such a thing, but her silly imagination had led her astray before. But maybe she had misinterpreted the scene at the depot.

Miss Opal glanced at Armilda across the breakfast table before addressing Lyna. "The young woman with the preacher was—"

"What is that noise?" Armilda cocked her head toward the back door.

The scratching noise continued, this time coupled with a sharp "yip."

"Oscar!" Lyna opened the screen door and scooped up the little dog. He was thin and dirty, and panting as if he had run a long way. "Where have you been, little dog?" Lyna cuddled him to her.

"Give the poor creature a drink, and then a bath please." Miss Opal wrinkled her nose.

"And then it's time for you to learn how to make biscuits, young lady." Armilda poked at the biscuit-rocks on her plate. "If you're going to marry the—"

Miss Opal cleared her throat loudly.

Lyna carried the dog over to the washtub and plopped him in it. "You stay there while I fetch the water. No more running away from home." She had missed the little creature.

"No more running away from home." *Wait. What was Armilda talking about?* Lyna raised her eyebrows. Had Miss Armilda almost said what she thought she had a minute ago? And when had Lyna ever said anything about getting married?

"As I was saying." Armilda adjusted her glasses. "When you get married someday, you'll need to know how to make biscuits your man will eat."

"Yes, ma'am. Mama never could quite get the hang of making biscuits." Lyna scrubbed Oscar's little head.

Are we discussing biscuits or marriage?

Armilda sniffed. "Well, in this house, we love fluffy biscuits. And the preacher does, too. Why, I've seen him eat six in one sitting."

Back to the preacher. So they were discussing marriage. *To Andrew?*

Lyna pictured him in the Wilsons' sunny kitchen, sitting in front of a mound of fluffy biscuits, happily slathering them with butter and dewberry jam. For him, she could learn how to bake. Maybe.

"I guess I'd better learn how to make fluffy biscuits." Lyna glanced at her elderly friends as she poured water over the dog's sudsy back. Could Miss Armilda have meant that she, Lyna Marshall, should marry Andrew? Maybe the woman at the train station wasn't anyone special after all.

Oscar shivered pitifully, more from fright than from cold. It had to be about 100 degrees in this kitchen by now. With the oven blazing and the cloudless heat of a Texas day in August, even the sisters' fancy electric fans were hardly helping.

"At least the dog will dry quickly in this heat." She set him down and moved out of the way so he could shake. Too bad she couldn't shake off her own confused thoughts that easily.

She sighed at the thought of more cooking lessons when she longed to lose herself in the wonderland of the library, but when Miss Armilda spoke, one listened. Unless one was Miss Opal, of course.

Lyna snickered inside. Over the past few weeks, she had developed a real fondness for the sisters, and she knew that under Opal's stern exterior was a heart of…of honey. But even for all that, anyone who knew Opal knew who was in charge.

"Did the preacher tell you he's headed to Dallas this week, Lyna?" Opal rose from the table.

"We talked for a minute in the kitchen last night." As far as Lyna knew, the sisters hadn't observed the pie incident, and she hoped to keep it that way.

"I see." Miss Opal's blue eyes twinkled. "He'll be leaving Moses in our barn while he's gone. I trust you won't mind caring for another horse for a few days."

If there was anything Lyna liked as well as playing the piano or reading a good novel, it was a horse. She missed her own mare, Cinnamon, and was glad she at least had the Wilsons' pair of bays to care for every day. It would be fun to get acquainted with Andrew's Moses.

"He'll be stopping by tomorrow before he leaves, so I told him he might as well stay for supper." "He said he had a story to tell us."

Andrew was coming over again? Tomorrow? How should she act around him? She had been quite sure he had wanted to say more to her last night, but Mrs. Olsen had waddled into the kitchen right at that moment. The magic spell shattered. What would have happened if—

"He said he had a story to tell us."

"A story?" Lyna mopped up the water around the washtub.

"Yes, whenever he comes back from his circuit, he always tells us about it. Sometimes he even preaches us his sermon if we ask him to enough times."

Lyna smiled to herself. The old dears were smitten with Andrew, and she didn't blame them one bit.

"I'd ride along with him if I was a little younger," Armilda said. "A little adventure is good for the soul."

****

And Andrew had had quite an adventure, they all agreed later, after hearing his harrowing tale over Miss Armilda's chicken and dumplings.

"God must have sent a whole division of angels to protect me." Andrew laid his napkin down.

"Or just one or two small ones who were really good shots." Miss Opal gave Armilda a meaningful glance.

Lyna's eyes were shining. "Oh, I wish I could have been there! I've always wanted to see an angel!"

She wished she would have been there? She had spunk, that was for sure.

Andrew chuckled. "I didn't actually see any angels. But I somehow felt their protection…I knew I would make it through. I guess God's not finished with me yet, after all."

Armilda sniffed. "What do you mean, 'after all,' Preacher?"

Uh, oh. If he didn't fix things quick, he was in for one of the sisters' sermons. And they could pack quite a wallop, those sermons could. Out of the corner of his eye, he saw Miss Opal reaching for her Bible. He gulped.

"Now, Miss Armilda, don't get your feathers all ruffled," he said. "I'm not abandoning my calling. I'm just … restless." He squirmed under the alert gazes of three pairs of female eyes. He might as well go for broke. "I know God brought me down here, and that I have work to do here. But lately I've been sensing that He is leading me in a new direction."

"Well, hallelujah!" Miss Opal put on her glasses. "What is it?"

"Ah. Therein lies the problem. I don't know yet, exactly. But I'm hoping to gain some direction after I talk to 'Mr. Salvation Army' in Dallas this week."

Lyna leaned toward him. "I've heard of the Salvation Army! Why do they call him that?"

Andrew shrugged. "Apparently, he first started preaching on the street corners in his red Salvation Army uniform way back in 1888. Some people don't think he has any other clothes than that. But he's doing an amazing work there."

He couldn't read the look on Lyna's face. Was she thinking of her preacher-grandfather? He knew how deeply she admired the man.

Opal and Armilda were nodding and smiling at both of them. He looked from one to the other, but didn't get any answers.

"You'd better eat. Your dumplings will get cold." Armilda gestured toward his plate.

He tucked his napkin into his collar more firmly and picked up his fork. At least he had avoided a sermon. And his dumplings *were* getting cold, but he might as well forge on ahead at this point.

He cleared his throat. "And the other problem, of course, is Margaret," he said.

The room went silent, except for the ticking of the grandfather clock in the parlor. He set his fork down. Had he said something wrong? It was not often that Miss Opal was speechless.

"Yes, well, I'm sure that particular…situation… will be worked out before too long." Miss Opal raised her eyebrows in a manner that Andrew assumed meant she was trying to tell him something significant. Unfortunately, he was not very schooled in the nuances of womanly communication.

"May I ask who Margaret is?" Lyna's voice was quiet.

Andrew pinched the bridge of his nose. This was getting way more complicated than simple dinner conversation. And what was he to say to Lyna? She must know by now that he—that he what? Had feelings for her? Was falling in love with her?

"Margaret thinks she is going to marry the preacher, Lyna." Miss Opal stared hard at Andrew.

Lyna's eyes widened and she turned to him. "She *thinks* she is?"

Andrew grimaced. "Margaret is an old family friend. She…we…I promised her father I would marry her this year."

Miss Opal and Miss Armilda were shaking their heads in unison.

"She's the wrong one, Preacher." Miss Opal always put her glasses on when things were getting serious, and now she stared him down over the top of the wire frames.

"Clearly. But—" *What? Had he just admitted out loud that Margaret would be unsuitable for him? But then what? He couldn't just go back on his word. He had promised—*

"God will provide a way," Miss Opal said in her preaching voice, raising her Bible high in both hands. "Just as He delivered you from the robbers by Little River, he can deliver you from—"

"Your sling is slipping," Armilda said blandly.

****

Later, Andrew could never quite remember how the rest of the evening had come about. Maybe he was dazed by the sparkle in Lyna's eye. Or maybe it was the cookies she had made for dessert. He wasn't quite sure, having never done any baking himself, but it seemed that cookies in general should not be bitter, nor have powdery little white spots all over them. But she had looked so pleased with herself that he had manfully plowed through four of the awful things. At least he had plenty of Miss Opal's sweet tea to wash it all down the best he could.

He had taken Lyna's small hand in his as he left the Wilson's that night, and attempted to ignore Miss Opal, who was lurking in the parlor.

"I wasn't trying to hide my relationship with Margaret from you, Lyna." He gazed into those green, green eyes. "Up until last night in the kitchen, I didn't think there was any real reason to tell you about her."

"What *did* happen last night, Andrew?"

He darted a glance toward the parlor. "Let's take a stroll out to the barn, shall we? You and Moses haven't been properly introduced."

Oscar scooted out under their feet as Andrew opened the front door.

Andrew shut the door behind them. The humid darkness settled around them as they ambled back to the Wilsons' barn, and Andrew tried to pretend he had not seen the kitchen curtain moving. He held the lantern high as he pushed open the door to the small barn, and Lyna giggled as she passed through under his outstretched arm.

"Did you see Miss Opal holding up her Bible? I don't think there's truly anything wrong with her arm, is there?"

Andrew chuckled. "No, I don't think so. I think those two have been plotting something for a long time."

Lyna smiled into his eyes. "And did the plot work?"

He set the lantern down to take both of her hands in his.

"I think it did." His mouth went dry. "I don't know how all of this is going to end, Lyna, but I know Margaret could never be the person who would walk this kind of life with me. I finally realized that once and for all this morning when I got another letter from her." He gave into his yearning then, and cupped Lyna's soft cheek—the one with the dimple—in his hand. "And then last night—"

She leaned into his touch. "It was the pie, wasn't it," she murmured. "I knew it. Mama always told me—"

He laughed out loud and pulled her into his embrace. How did she always manage to catch him off guard? "It was the pie, for sure, Lyna." He tucked her head comfortably under his chin. "When that pie hit my leg, I just knew, then and there, that you were …"

He pulled back to search her eyes, and the air left his lungs. Was this the woman God had planned for him all along? This lovely soul, who laughed easily and forgave quickly? Who dreamed impossible dreams? Who loved God with a passion to match his own? Who he somehow knew would stand by him come hell or high water?

"Andrew."

In the dimness, he was surprised to see tears glinting in her eyes.

"What is it, sweetheart?" He rubbed his thumb across her cheek.

"Can't you feel it?" She laid her small hand against his chest, right where his heart threatened to pound through. "It's like our souls are—"

Andrew felt the great whoosh of hot horse breath a second before Moses forced his head between the two of them.

"Well." Andrew stepped back. "Now you know why his name is Moses. He loves to lay down the law."

He couldn't see her past the horse's head, but he heard her giggle. A crazy grin stretched across his face. Life with Lyna would never be dull.

Epilogue

Dear Miss Opal Wilson,

I am pleased to accept your quite unexpected and generous sponsorship to the Boston Conservatory of Music. Papa always said taking bassoon lessons would pay off! However, since I will surely be spending the majority of my time performing concerts for high society functions here in Boston, I regret to inform you that I will not be returning to Texas as planned. Please tell Andrew that I received his letter and I wish him well in his efforts. Thank you for your solicitous inquiries about my plans over the past few weeks, and I do hope both you and your charming sister are back up to full and vigorous health as you were during my lovely visit earlier this summer.

Fondly,
Miss Margaret Rushford

****

Miss Opal moved the lace curtains a smidge, just enough to see the preacher and his new bride strolling hand in hand through the daisy patch.

"Well," said Opal. "That plan went off real fine, if I do say so myself. And to think Andrew and Lyna will be opening up a rescue mission, right here in Belton." She peeked out at the couple again and sighed. "It just warms the cockles of my heart."

Armilda stood at the sideboard, crimping the edge of a pie crust. She sniffed. "Next time, I'm speaking to the Lord about things on my own."

"Next time?" Opal stowed her cane behind the back door.

Armilda rolled her eyes. "There is *always* a next time with you, Opal Wilson. Always."

Opal smiled. She would have to see what the good Lord thought about that.

Miss Opal's Favorite
SCOTTISH FANCIES

from *The Boston Cooking School Cookbook*
by Fannie Farmer, 2nd edition, 1906

1 egg	1 cup rolled oats
1/2 cup sugar	1/3 teaspoon salt
2/3 tablespoon melted butter	1/4 teaspoon vanilla

Beat egg until light, add gradually sugar, and then stir in remaining ingredients. Drop mixture by teaspoonfuls on a thoroughly greased inverted dripping-pan one inch apart. Spread into circular shape with a case knife first dipped in cold water. Bake in a moderate oven until delicately browned. To give variety use two-thirds cup rolled oats and fill cup with shredded coconut.

Bell County, Texas

Bell County was founded in 1850 and named for Peter Hansborough Bell, the third governor of Texas. Its county seat is Belton. In 1907, when Miss Opal "lived" in Belton, the town boasted a courthouse, a library, an opera house, several churches, a community swimming pool, two cotton-seed oil mills, and many other businesses.

First Baptist Church of Belton

First Baptist Church of Belton was founded in 1853 with a group of eight people. Today, FBC Belton is home to a large and thriving congregation. It is still on Main Street and continues to be an integral part of the Belton community.

About the Author

Amy Rognlie lives in Bell County, Texas with her husband, their youngest son and two dogs. They also have two grown sons and one granddaughter. After living in Colorado for many years, Amy is now a "transplanted" Texan, and is enjoying the new friends, new adventures and renewed faith that God has brought into her life in the past few years.

Amy loves learning and is especially fascinated with the history of her new state. She wishes Miss Opal was around to tell her more stories, but instead, she'll have to come up with more on her own. Like the time Miss Opal was elected as president of the Ladies Missionary Aid Society and …

Also by Amy K. Rognlie:

Along Unfamiliar Paths (Barbour Books)
After the Flowers Fade (Barbour Books)
A Vow Unbroken in *The Bartered Bride Collection*
(Barbour Books)

Visit Amy on her Facebook page:
https://www.facebook.com/AmyRognlie

Website:
arognlie.wixsite.com/texasauthor